The
Bizarre
History of
Beauty

BRUTAL
BODY BINDING
AND MODIFICATION

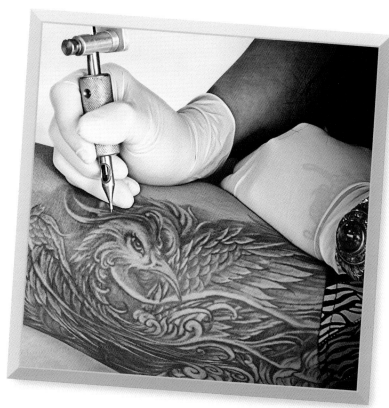

ANITA CROY

Gareth Stevens
PUBLISHING

Please visit our website, www.garethstevens.com.
For a free color catalog of all our high-quality books,
call toll free 1-800-542-2595 or fax 1-877-542-2596.

Cataloging-in-Publication Data
Names: Croy, Anita.
Title: Brutal body binding and modification / Anita Croy.
Description: New York : Gareth Stevens Publishing, 2019. | Series: The bizarre history of beauty | Includes glossary and index.
Identifiers: ISBN 9781538226834 (pbk.) | ISBN 9781538226827 (library bound)
Subjects: LCSH: Human body–Social aspects–Juvenile literature. | Body image–Juvenile literature. | Body marking–Juvenile literature.
Classification: LCC GT495.C79 2019 | DDC 306.4–dc23

First Edition

Published in 2019 by
Gareth Stevens Publishing
111 East 14th Street, Suite 349
New York, NY 10003

© 2019 Gareth Stevens Publishing

Produced for Gareth Stevens by Calcium
Editors: Sarah Eason and Tim Cooke
Designers: Clare Webber and Lynne Lennon
Picture researcher: Rachel Blount

Picture credits: Cover: Shutterstock: Yu Zhang; Inside: Library of Congress: B.J. Falk: p. 33; Shutterstock: Axel Bueckert: p. 43; Charcompix: pp. 1, 42; Chrisdorney: p. 12; Elnur: p. 38; Everett Historical: pp. 27, 32; Gurprit.s13: p. 20; Anastasiia Kazakova: p. 35; Litvinov: p. 39b; Lucky Business: p. 40; Mnimage: p. 37b; Pixelheadphoto digitalskillet: p. 41; Poznyakov: p. 39t; Yu Zhang: p. 15t; Sofia Zhuravetc: p. 9b; Wikimedia Commons: pp. 22, 37t; Lai Afong: p. 14; John Atherton: p. 10; George Barbier: p. 34; D. Bernard & Co, Melbourne/Wellcome Images: p. 36; John de Critz: p. 18; restoration and digitization Didier Descouens: pp. 6, 7; Jan van Eyck: p. 19; Luke Fildes: p. 25t; Kathy Gerber: p. 11; Gianfranco Gori: p. 21t; Steven van Herwijck: p. 13; Workshop of Hans Holbein the Younger: p. 17; Georg Heinrich von Langsdorff: p. 24; Gottfried Lindauer: p. 21b; Los Angeles County Museum of Art: p. 29; Henry Robert Morland: p. 30; Thilo Parg: p. 4; PD: p. 28; Yves Picq: p. 23; Parkinson, Sydney: p. 5t; Daniel Schwen: p. 15b; William Scrots: p. 16; James Steakley: p. 26; The Plaza Gallery, Los Angeles: p. 25b; Tovar, Juan de: p. 8; U.S. National Archives and Records Administration: p. 9t; Michel Wal: p. 5b; Wellcome Image: p. 31.

All rights reserved. No part of this book may be reproduced in any form without permission from the publisher, except by a reviewer.

Printed in the United States of America

CPSIA compliance information: Batch #CS18GS:
For further information contact Gareth Stevens, New York, New York at 1-800-542-2595.

-CONTENTS-

Chapter 1
THE ANCIENT
- WORLD -

Since the times of the earliest humans, people have often deliberately modified the appearance or shape of their bodies in both permanent and temporary ways.

In 1991, walkers high in the Alps in Austria stumbled across the frozen body of a man in the ice. The body had been exposed by a melting **glacier**. When scientists examined the body, they discovered it was more than 5,000 years old. Ötzi the Iceman, as they nicknamed him, lived around 3300 BC.

IT'S NOT A NEW LOOK!

Ötzi's body was covered in around 58 **tattoos**. Most of them were over his bone joints, which led scientists to think he suffered from a painful condition called **arthritis**. The tattoos might have been intended to be some kind of magic protection against the condition. Ötzi is the oldest example of **body modification** ever discovered, but there is plenty of other evidence that the practice was common. Such evidence includes tattooed figures painted on rocks in Saharan caves and tattooed ancient Egyptian **mummies** who died around 2000 BC.

Ötzi the Iceman, seen here in a model showing how he probably looked, had tattoos over his body joints.

CHANGING SHAPE

Ancient humans did not just tattoo their bodies. They also deliberately cut, scarred, and pierced their faces and bodies. The reasons for altering the body were religious, social, and cultural. They varied widely from culture to culture. The use of scarification—the creation of patterns of scars in the skin—was seen as being beautiful by some African peoples but as horrific by others. In ancient Mexico, kings and **nobles** left scars when they pierced their bodies and tongues with cactus spines to draw blood to offer to the ancient gods. When Captain James Cook arrived in Polynesia in the eighteenth century, he was shocked by the tattooed faces of the peoples he met. At the time, there was no equivalent in Europe.

What scarring and tattooing had in common was that they hurt—and they were irreversible. Other changes were less painful and more temporary. In medieval Europe, for example, women wore their hair in styles that made their skulls appear longer, because they believed it made them look more intelligent. A longer skull meant more room for the memory!

In New Zealand, the Maori tattooed designs on their faces.

This Mayan carving from Mexico shows a noble piercing his tongue (right).

DON'T BE
- A BIGHEAD! -

Many ancient cultures did not think much of humans' naturally round heads. Some peoples thought elongated skulls were much more attractive.

The earliest people we know changed the shape of their heads were the Chinchorro who lived in present-day Chile in South America between 7000 and 2000 BC. They flattened their foreheads and squeezed their skulls into an elongated cone by wrapping their heads in tight headbands made from camel hair.

SO LONG BABY!

The bands were so tight that the Chinchorros' skulls changed over their lives into distinctive long heads. Later, the Maya of Central America and the Inca of Peru believed the gods preferred long skulls because they appeared more noble. For that reason, those peoples only allowed members of the ruling classes to change the shape of their heads. Ordinary people were stuck to leave their heads as they were.

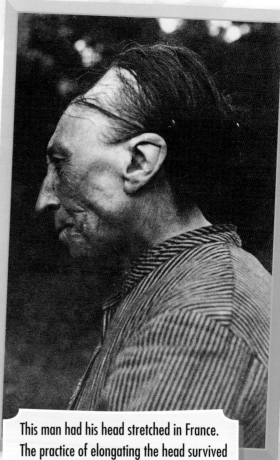

This man had his head stretched in France. The practice of elongating the head survived in a tiny area into the twentieth century.

A number of North American tribes also flattened their babies' skulls. Around AD 1000, the Anasazi people of the Southwest tied their babies to wooden boards that pressed against the soft skull, changing its shape.

HOW'S IT DONE?

When babies are born, the bones in their skulls are soft. As they age, the bones harden. To change the shape of a skull, the infant's skull was tightly wrapped in cloth bandages. Some cultures placed wooden boards against the back and sides of the head. Over time, the shape of the skull changed. Because the bandages and boards stopped it from growing outward, it grew longer. Once the shape changed, there was no way to change it back. In some cultures, long heads were a way to show off your wealth! Poor people always had round heads.

This elongated skull came from Peru, where members of the Incas' ruling class changed the shape of their heads.

to die for

Although it may look strange, elongating a baby's skull did not actually harm the baby. As long as the brain was not damaged and it had room to grow as large as a normal brain, the child would grow up without any loss of brain function. You might think they looked like an alien from outer space—but they wouldn't act like one!

PIERCING

Piercing holes in different parts of the body to hold ornaments is probably the best known and most popular form of body modification.

Today, everyone knows someone with pierced ears. However, piercings are nearly as old as humans. Almost every part of the body can be and has been pierced.

MANY PIERCINGS

The Aztec of Mexico pierced their bodies with cactus spines. They believed the supply of fresh blood kept their gods happy— which meant the gods would keep the universe alive. The Maya, meanwhile, jabbed needles made from stingray spines through their ears, cheeks, lips, tongues, and other body parts to mark important **milestones** in life. That must have hurt!

Aztec priests carry out a ritual to ask the gods for rain. Such rituals often included body piercing.

THAT DOESN'T HURT!

Ancient peoples took pride in not displaying pain when their bodies were pierced. Body piercing was a central part of Native American culture. The Sun Dance ceremony was one of the most sacred rituals of the Plains peoples. Young men pierced their chests and then danced around the sacred pole attached to it by cords joined to their piercings. To deaden the pain, the warriors entered a **trance** before their bodies were pierced. Who knows how much that helped?

Shoshone warriors perform the Sun Dance. They were attached to a pole by cords joined to piercings in their chests.

to die for

Ear piercings are so common today that we rarely think twice about them. Ear piercing is one of the most ancient forms of body modification. Ötzi the Iceman had a pierced ear. Pierced ears have been in fashion for almost all of history. However, they did fall briefly out of fashion at the start of the twentieth century, when clip-on earrings were all the rage.

Pierced ears are traditional for both male and female followers of Hinduism in India.

SCARIFICATION

Imagine your body was a book that recorded important details about your life and your tribe. That's the purpose of scarification.

Today, inked tattoos are a fairly common way that some people choose to change the look of their skin. But throughout history, some people have used another method, called scarification.

TELL ME ABOUT YOU

In Africa, different tribes have decorated their faces and bodies with a wide variety of designs for thousands of years. These scars are not just for decoration, however. The designs contain lots of information about the individual. Scars record the important milestones in a person's life, such as becoming an adult or getting married. Other scars show which tribe a person belongs to. Scars come in all shapes and sizes, from **incisions** to complex patterns of raised scars known as keloids. To some peoples, scarring is a sign of beauty.

This pattern of scarification was created by incising lines into the flesh in a regular pattern.

CUT AWAY

To create a scar, people pull up the skin and use knives to cut it away. They then push soot or ground charcoal into the wound, which both raises the scar and stops infections in the wound. The more the skin is pulled away from the flesh before it is cut, the higher the keloid will be. A high keloid is considered much more attractive than a flatter one.

In some cultures, getting their first scars is an important moment for young children. As their skin is cut into to create a design, they do not make a sound. Proving they can stand the pain is an important way to show everyone just how brave they are. Once made, the scar is permanent. It will be added to as the child grows up and goes through life.

This Datoga woman from Tanzania has two parallel circles of keloids around her eyes.

Chapter 2

THE MIDDLE
- AGES -

Are you highbrow or lowbrow? That was the burning question in the Middle Ages. Only the wealthy could afford to change how they looked. The poor were stuck with what they had.

The Emperor Constantine ruled the Roman Empire in the early fourth century AD. During his reign, Christianity became the most important religion across Europe and the Near East.

THE HEIGHT OF FASHION

As Christianity spread, body modification came to be associated with the lowest classes of society. Constantine banned tattoos. They were worn only by criminals, who were branded as a form of punishment, and by pagans, who did not follow Christianity. Without tattoos or piercings to decorate the body, medieval people used clothes to change the shapes of their bodies. Men wore short jackets with over-padded shoulders to make their waists appear slimmer. Their **doublets** stopped at the knees to emphasize their slim calves.

Constantine was the first Roman emperor to become a Christian. He banned the use of tattoos.

Medieval men used a tight tunic and puffed-up doublet to make their waists appear as small as possible.

BREATHE IN!

It was a bit tougher being a medieval woman. Being slim was in fashion. If women had eaten too much or were naturally heavy, they could use a tight-fitting conical V-shaped **bodice**. The garment was tied around the torso to pull in the waist. From the early fourteenth century, bodices were stiffened with paste. Later they were made with whalebone. This was a substance that actually came from whale teeth and formed stiff spokes inside the bodice.

Looking smart was also fashionable, and in the medieval world a large expanse of forehead equaled intelligence. Women pulled their hair off their faces and tucked it into high headdresses. They shaved off their eyebrows, making them appear instantly "highbrow." They were easy to tell apart from the "lowbrow" peasants with their eyebrows and uncovered hair.

TINY
- FEET -

In medieval China, the most desirable brides had feet no bigger than a doll's foot. Although it was painful and disabling, the practice of foot binding lasted for 1,000 years.

According to legend, Yao Niang was a dancer at the court of Emperor Li Yu in the tenth century. Yao Niang bound her feet into the shape of the new moon. The emperor loved her feet so much that a new fashion was born overnight among the court ladies.

I CAN'T WALK!

With time and money on their hands, ladies at court set out to shrink their feet until they were so tiny they were almost impossible to walk on. By the thirteenth century, some women's feet were so tiny they looked more like those of a miniature doll. Small feet were the height of fashion. In order to be effective, foot binding had to start at an early age. The girl had to be no more than five or six years old—before she had any real choice in the matter.

Lai Afong, a Chinese **courtier**, displays her tiny feet.

LOTUS FEET

The process took two years and was very painful. To begin with, all the toes were broken except the big toe, which was needed for balance when walking. The foot was bent over and bound with silk strips, which were changed often to avoid infection. Over time, the wrapping was pulled tighter and tighter as the sole and heel were crushed together. The most highly prized foot was a "golden **lotus**." Just 3 inches (7.5 cm) long, it guaranteed a marriage proposal. The "silver lotus" was an acceptable 4 inches (10 cm), but a 5-inch (12.5 cm) "iron lotus" foot was a failure. If you changed your mind and decided you wanted normal feet, too bad! The process could not be reversed.

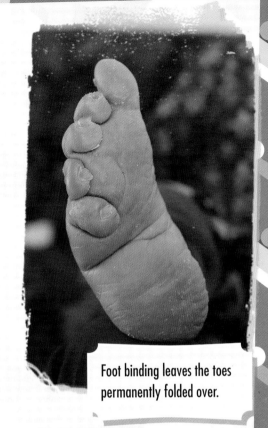

Foot binding leaves the toes permanently folded over.

hello beautiful

Lady Huang Sheng, the wife of a member of the emperor's family in China, died in 1243. When she was buried, her tiny feet were wrapped in gauze. They were then placed inside a pair of tiny silk lotus shoes that were small enough to fit into a human hand.

Lotus shoes are tiny slippers made of silk.

SO
- MACHO -

For the sixteenth-century man about town, showing off his body was a top priority. He used his clothes to do the talking.

Edward VI became king of England in 1547 at age nine. His stuffed doublet disguised the fact that he was a sickly boy. He died just six years later.

Every man wanted to look fit and healthy—the equivalent of a gym-goer today—with a broad chest, narrow waist, and slender legs. However, few men were prepared to put in the work to achieve that masculine shape.

A QUESTION OF SIZE

Instead, men wore special tunics stuffed with **bombast**. A man's doublet or tunic was stuffed with up to 5–6 pounds (2–3 kg) of rags, horsehair, cotton, and bran to swell its size. This gave the wearer an instant chest of mammoth proportions—but there was a downside. If the doublet leaked, the bran trickled out. The bombast was so heavy that many men complained of having sore backs. Another problem was that **lice** often infested the bran.

EVER-CHANGING TRENDS

Like all fashion trends, the styles of men's doublets and jackets changed over time. During some points in history, they were generally longer and sometimes included a skirted portion that covered the thighs. However, by the sixteenth century, men's doublets or jackets had grown fatter and shorter. To accompany their doublets, men usually wore tight-fitting woollen or silk stockings, called hose, to show off their muscular legs. At the time, it was considered fashionable for men to show off the shape of their legs. It was especially common for upper-class men to wear tight-fitting hose. Breeches were also a common type of pants that men of this time period often wore.

hello beautiful

One of the biggest fans of the stuffed doublet was the sixteenth-century King Henry VIII of England. To make him look powerful, Hans Holbein the Younger painted Henry with his chest suitably puffed out (thanks to the bombast stuffing). His manly chest and toned legs were shown off to their best effect. Later in his life, Henry gained quite a bit of weight.

Henry VIII was painted as the model of a shapely, fashionable Tudor man.

FEMALE
- SILHOUETTES -

In the sixteenth century women began to squeeze into clothes that altered their natural shape. Women's fashion would never be the same again.

For most of history, women's clothes had followed the shape of their bodies. That was no longer the case. New fashions set out to alter women's shapes.

A BIG SQUEEZE

Toward the end of the sixteenth century, fashionable women started wearing a new item of clothing to change their shape. They wore stiff boards in the front of their dresses. These boards, called stomachers, were like early versions of the **corset**. Shaped like an upside-down triangle, they squeezed in women's ribs and waists. That made breathing a little tricky. The upside was that stomachers made waists look tiny. The stomachers were covered in beautiful embroidered silk, so they looked striking. The trend took off. It lasted into the eighteenth century.

In this painting from around 1601, Princess Anne of Denmark wears a stomacher and a farthingale to create the ideal narrow waist.

IT'S A CINCH

Having a tiny waist became the ideal shape for a woman. Wealthy women emphasized their narrow waists by wearing extremely wide skirts called farthingales. A farthingale was a framework of circular bands made from steel or whalebone that held the skirt away from the woman's legs in a shape resembling a bell. The skirts became so large that women could only sit down by perching on the edge of a seat. Queen Elizabeth I of England, Henry VIII's daughter, was a huge fan, so the **voluminous** skirts became popular at the English court. Farthingales and stomachers made it impossible to tell what a woman really looked like. That made sense. The original farthingale was designed to hide the unwanted pregnancy of Queen Juana of Portugal in 1470.

hello beautiful

In this famous portrait, the wife of Giovanni di Nicolao Arnolfini wears a long dress belted high up beneath her chest and pats her stomach. For years, experts assumed the woman—we do not know her name—was pregnant. In fact, she was not pregnant, but fashionable! Having lots of material gathered at the front was the style at the time.

Jan van Eyck painted *The Arnolfini Marriage* in 1434. It likely shows an Italian merchant and his wife.

Chapter 3
THE EARLY
-MODERN AGE-

*From the fifteenth century,
Europeans set sail to explore the world. They
were looking for new sea routes to the sources of
the spices that were so highly prized in Europe.*

On their voyages, explorers encountered all kinds of people. They returned to Europe with news of the strange appearances of some of the peoples they met.

AROUND THE WORLD

Different peoples around the world use body modification as part of their culture. Among the first practices was lip stretching. It is at least 10,000 years old and is still practiced in parts of Africa. A girl's lower lip was pierced and a peg inserted to stretch it. When the lip was stretched, a bigger peg or flat disk was inserted. A stretched lip was a sign of beauty—as long as it didn't break. If a girl's lip broke, she would never find a husband. In India, meanwhile, women pierced their left nostrils. According to the ancient Indian **Ayurvedic** tradition of medicine, the left nostril was associated with **fertility**.

Indian women pierced their left nostrils in the belief that it would increase their chances of having a baby.

In ancient India, brides-to-be painted their hands with **mehndi**. These complicated designs were like tattoos, but they were made with a dye called henna. Unlike tattoos, mehndi eventually washes off. In the Pacific region, meanwhile, tattooing was an important part of life and full of symbolism. For the Maori, face tattoos were used as a personal signature. When Maori chiefs signed legal contracts with Europeans, they drew their face tattoos instead of writing their names.

This girl from a tribe in Ethiopia has enlarged earlobes and a lower lip stretched around a disk.

BACK HOME

Early Europeans failed to understand the social and cultural significance of tattoos. They thought native peoples' lack of clothes and painted bodies showed they were savages. According to Christian ideas, any sort of face painting and body adornment was a form of **vanity**—and therefore a sin. As Europeans took control of vast parts of the world, they outlawed native practices. In the Pacific region and Africa, Christian **missionaries** fought to halt the practice of tattooing. They even used pieces of coral to scrape off people's tattoos. That procedure was probably even more painful than having the tattoo in the first place!

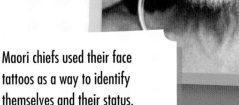

Maori chiefs used their face tattoos as a way to identify themselves and their status.

BODY
-ALTERATION-

European travelers encountered peoples with enlarged lips, elongated necks, and earlobes that dangled to their shoulders. It was unlike anything they had ever seen.

One body alteration found around the world was piercing the ears to wear ornaments. Ancient cultures believed demons and spirits entered the body through the ears. The first earrings were charms to prevent this from happening.

BODY PIERCING

In Europe, sailors began a male fashion by wearing gold earrings (they also started the craze for tattoos). It was said that the value of the earrings was used to pay for a funeral if they died at sea. Soon, fashionable men in England wore a single earring in their left ear. The fashion statement quickly caught on and soon no self-respecting courtier of Queen Elizabeth I would let themselves be seen without an earring.

The English playwright William Shakespeare had his portrait painted in 1610 wearing a gold hoop in his ear.

NECK STRETCHING

In southeast Asia, Europeans met tribal women who wore iron hoops to stretch their necks. The rings, which weighed up to 25 pounds (11.4 kg), were put on a young girl at the age of about five. No one really knows why the practice began, but it may have reflected the tribespeople's idea of beauty. In fact, the rings did not actually elongate the neck. Instead, they pressed down the collarbone and ribs, making the neck appear longer. Similarly, other tribes elongated their lips and earlobes by stretching them with pegs and disks that grew gradually larger. In parts of Africa, extended lips are still considered very attractive.

The Karen people of Myanmar still follow the tradition of elongating their necks.

to die for

Stories about the differing appearance of people around the world spread through Europe. The tales of enlarged lips and long necks soon became exaggerated. Some accounts reported a group of people who walked on their hands. Other people were said to have no heads, but eyes and mouths on their torsos!

TATTOO
- YOU -

When the British sailor James Cook arrived in the Pacific region in 1769, he discovered a whole culture of people whose skin was decorated with tattoos.

The word *tattoo* comes from the Polynesian word *tatau*, which means "to write." Polynesians wrote on their skin instead of on paper. The Europeans had no idea what the tattoos meant.

WRITTEN ON THE SKIN

Tattoos described everything about a Polynesian, from what island he or she came from to the individual's family and his or her position within it. Tattoos also recorded all the important milestones in a person's life, such as reaching adulthood or having a child. The Polynesians used chisels made from bones or shells to apply ink beneath the surface of the skin. Captain Cook and other Europeans who encountered the different Polynesian bands had no idea the tattoos meant anything. For them, tattoos were a sign of vanity that went against the teachings of the Bible. They took no notice of the fact that the Polynesians had their own religion that was very different from Christianity!

Some Polynesians covered their whole body with tattoos, shocking European visitors.

TATTOOS AWAY

Tattoos were among the many exotic imports early explorers brought home with them. Sailors, in particular, liked the idea— but they did not get much beyond simple designs. The first tattoo parlor opened in London in 1870 and tattoos became fashionable in Europe—just as Christian missionaries were killing off the art in Polynesia. In Great Britain, tattoos became socially acceptable in the late nineteenth century after the Duke of York, a sailor, had a small dragon tattooed on his arm during a trip to Japan in 1881. If royal princes could have a tattoo, so could anyone!

The Duke of York became King George V in 1911—and the first British king with a tattoo.

hello beautiful

Eighty years ago, few Americans had a tattoo—and virtually no women. A few women had the idea of making a living by tattooing their bodies. One of the most famous was Betty Broadbent, who appeared at fairs as the "Tattoo'd Lady." Her body was covered with 565 tattoos! In 1981, she became the first person to be inducted into the Tattoo Hall of Fame.

Maud Stevens Wagner claimed to be the first "tattooed lady" in the United States.

Chapter 4

THE NINETEENTH
- CENTURY -

In the early nineteenth century, the Romantic movement swept across Europe. People turned to diet and exercise to create bodies that suited the fashions of the day.

The first gym opened 5,000 years ago in ancient Crete to help men build up their strength for battle. For the ancient Greeks and Romans, gyms were places to both exercise and meet your friends. In the Middle Ages, any serious knight had to ride, wrestle, and swim to keep fit.

PUMPING IRON

In 1811, Friedrich Ludwig Jahn opened the first modern gym in Berlin in Prussia (modern Germany). He thought exercise would help restore battered Prussian pride after a defeat by the French. Jahn believed physical exercise improved not only the body but also the mind.

Men exercise at a gymnasium in Milwaukee, Wisconsin, in the nineteenth century.

A full skirt and a narrow waist was the ideal body shape for nineteenth-century women.

The idea soon caught on in the United States. In 1817 the first gym opened at the military academy in West Point. At the time, gyms were only for the boys. One women's magazine, *Godey's Lady's Book*, suggested that the best form of exercise for women was doing the housework!

THIN AND PALE

While some people were pumping iron, others were deliberately going without food. **Romanticism** made it fashionable to be pale and thin—and even a little sickly. Many women starved themselves so they could live up to the ideal—and possibly even attract the attention of the dashing Romantic hero, the poet Lord Byron. Byron spent years starving himself to make himself slim, and he exercised like a demon. For those who wanted to get the look but skip the exercise, vinegar was the drink of choice. Byron claimed that a diet of potatoes and vinegar kept him slim.

WHERE ARE
- THE LEGS? -

In nineteenth-century Britain, showing off your legs was a definite no-no. Both women and men dressed to hide their bodies beneath layers of clothing.

For nineteenth-century women, a narrow waist was everything—the smaller the better. Large skirts helped make waists look more slender.

SHE FLOATS

A Victorian woman had to be a weightlifter! She wore up to 30 pounds (13.6 kg) of clothing. Outfits weighed so much because they had layers and layers of material. A lady wore up to 10 **petticoats** as underskirts. Over them went a **crinoline**, which was a cagelike frame to create a circular shape, and then the dress itself. With so many petticoats, women could only take small steps. Because their dresses hid their feet, it looked as if they were gliding across the floor.

Even children's clothes disguised the natural shapes of their bodies.

PUT THOSE LEGS AWAY

In the middle of the seventeenth century, men had briefly had their own version of the farthingale and crinoline. They wore a new kind of leg covering known as Rhinegraves. They were named for a German nobleman. Rhinegraves were a little like a very full but short divided skirt made up of layers and layers of material that were gathered at the knee. Men's thighs and the tops of their legs were completely hidden, although Rhinegraves did show off their calves. Rhinegraves fell out of favor rapidly when England's King Charles II stopped wearing them.

In the eighteenth century, men wore breeches that grew longer over time. Eventually, breeches covered the whole leg, and men replaced wearing hose with wearing socks. By the start of the nineteenth century, long pants that hid the entire leg had come into fashion. They never went out of fashion again.

to die for

Crinolines were an example of the folly of fashion. They made skirts so wide that they became impractical. Women could no longer walk through a doorway without turning sideways. They stopped traveling in carriages with their friends: two skirts was one too many! Some women even died when their wide skirts touched an open flame and caught on fire.

A crinoline was a cage formed by hoops of steel, whalebone, or cane supported by thick tapes.

BREATHE
- IN! -

Women had worn various types of corset with various names for centuries. The peak of corset use came during the mid-nineteenth century. Britain's young Queen Victoria never went without one.

Everyone wanted a thin waist, and the corset was the quickest way to get one—if you could stand the pain!

LACE ME UP!

Nearly every woman wore a corset. Fashionable hourglass figures called for a 22-inch (56 cm) waist. That's 16 inches (40 cm) smaller than the average female waist today. Corsets were like tubes that wrapped around the torso and laced at the back. Women had to be helped to put them on. It was impossible to lace up your own corset. The tighter the laces, the thinner the waist—and the more difficulty breathing! In 1874, corsets were blamed for causing 97 different health problems, including deformed ribs, a **misaligned** spine, and a displaced stomach and liver.

Wearing a corset meant that any sort of effort—like doing the laundry—left women hot and out of breath!

MALE VANITY

It wasn't only women who subjected themselves to chronic discomfort in the name of fashion. Toward the end of the eighteenth century, men squeezed themselves into corsets, too. The fashion soon died when some people claimed corseted men were cheating their way to slimness while other men were off pumping iron. But a nipped-in waist remained a male ideal, and jackets were cut to emphasize the slender waistline. It was not until the twentieth century that the focus left the male waistline and he could breathe more easily—that is, if his fashionable high, stiffened collar did not kill him. In 1888, a man in New York died after he fell asleep in his clothes. When his head tipped forward, his rigid collar choked him!

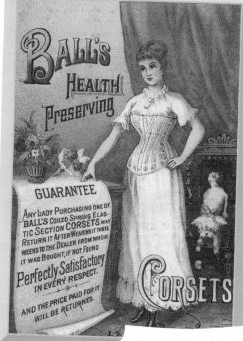

Although corsets were advertised as being good for the health, tight corsets could permanently damage the body.

to die for

The corset got a bad reputation for causing widespread fainting among Victorian women. Many people blamed the tight-laced corset for preventing the blood from circulating correctly. In fact, there were many reasons women may have passed out, including overheating from wearing so many layers and poisoning from the lead in their makeup.

THE FEMALE
- SHAPE -

Women were still not free to wear clothes that were comfortable. At the end of the nineteenth century, they were imprisoned in a steel frame once again.

When the crinoline fell out of fashion, it was replaced by the bustle. Instead of sticking out on either side, women's skirts and dresses now stuck out behind. This was seen as progress!

IT'S BACK

The bustle was a steel frame worn around the waist that protruded at the back. It used padding made from wires, springs, fabric, and **mohair** to add fullness to the back of the skirt, which was gathered in **pleats** of material. The bustle also made it almost impossible to sit down. It forced women to walk or stand, so they always looked busy. In fact, they "bustled." Just like the crinoline, the bustle could cause permanent damage to the body. Its weight pulled women's spines out of alignment.

Bustles pushed the body into what was known as an S-shape.

WAISTING AWAY

In the late nineteenth century, social pressure as well as the fashions of the day encouraged women to keep their waists as small as possible. It must have been difficult, because the Victorian and Edwardian eras were times when a greater variety of food became more widely available. Many people could afford to eat well—and they loved to eat!

Wealthy people enjoyed plenty of food, with three large meals a day as well as smaller meals throughout the day. It was the Victorians who introduced the three-course dinner: starter, main course, and dessert. Knowing they had to squeeze into their constricting corsets and skirts was enough to keep many Victorian and Edwardian ladies from stuffing themselves.

hello beautiful

Renowned English beauty and actress Lillie Langtry became famous for wearing bustles. Everyone wanted to look like her, so Lillie designed her own bustle, which was advertised in ladies' magazines. Its unique selling point was that it folded up when the wearer sat down, so she did not have to spend hours and hours bustling about.

Lillie Langtry invented a bustle that used hinges to fold up when a woman sat down.

Chapter 5
THE TWENTIETH
- CENTURY -

Clothing at the start of the twentieth century did not give much freedom to the wearer. Fashion continued to dictate and modify body shape.

Paul Poiret made his name with loose-fitting outfits that gave women's bodies freedom to move naturally.

As the century went on, however, social upheaval and growing freedom were eventually reflected in how people lived and how they treated their bodies.

I'M FREE!

In 1907, the French fashion designer Paul Poiret claimed to free women from the constraints of fashion. He put them in comfortable, loose **harem pants**. However, he then blew his claim by inventing the hobble skirt. This long skirt was so narrow at the ankles that women could barely move their feet. Their walk was reduced to a shuffle or hobble. Later, Poiret told women to ditch their corsets. Out went squeezing into the tight-laced garments and in came at least a little bit more freedom. Without corsets, many women could breathe easier!

SHOW IT OFF

Like the hobble skirt, many twentieth-century fashions were designed to accentuate the female form rather than for comfort or practicality. These fashions included the pencil skirt, a variation on the hobble skirt that made walking nearly impossible. Some of the century's fashions were just as cruel as ancient fashions had been.

Killer shoes with thin high heels have long been a fashion statement because they make women's legs look longer and slimmer. But **stiletto** shoes also distorted the feet, causing **bunions** and hip and leg problems. In the same way, both men and women squeezed their feet into narrow, pointed shoes for the sake of fashion. The winklepicker, worn in the 1950s, looked like the pointed shoes of the medieval era—and was no more comfortable.

From the moment many teenagers first wore blue jeans in the 1950s to copy the actor James Dean, jeans have been worn in all kinds of styles. In the 1980s, the fashion was for jeans so tight they looked as though they had been painted on. They sometimes stopped the blood's circulation around the body. Some women even had to be cut out of their skin-tight jeans.

High-heeled shoes and skinny jeans push the hips forward and emphasize the thinness of the legs.

BUILD THE
- BODY! -

The early twentieth century saw the rise of a new form of exercise: bodybuilding. Men, and a few women, set out to change their bodies by enlarging their muscles.

One hundred and fifty years ago, German bodybuilder Eugene Sandow created a new exercise regimen. It built up his muscles to transform his body into a strong, taut machine.

A LIVING STATUE

Sandow showed that it was possible to transform the body as he grew stronger and began taking part in strength competitions. Muscular men were so rare that Sandow was paid to show off his body at the 1893 World Exposition in Chicago. As well as being amazed by the weights he could lift, audiences loved poses that showed off his rippling muscles. In 1901, Sandow organized the first-ever bodybuilding competition in London. It was so successful people were turned away. Sandow's body had come to resemble an ancient Greek statue.

Eugene Sandow was the first man to deliberately use bodybuilding to try to change his body shape.

"HAVE A BODY LIKE MINE"

One man who cashed in on the public's enthusiasm to transform their bodies was an Italian American named Angelo Siciliano. Skinny and weak as a child, Siciliano decided to build up his body to look just like a statue of the Greek god Hercules in the local museum. Too poor to afford weights, Siciliano devised a routine that worked one muscle against another. Before long, he did look like a Greek god! His friends nicknamed him Atlas after the god the Greeks believed held Earth on his shoulders. Now calling himself Charles Atlas, he turned his bodybuilding technique into a multi-million-dollar business in the 1920s. Thousands of men followed Atlas's program, changing their bodies and growing stronger.

Charles Atlas became famous through magazine advertisements in the 1920s and 1930s.

to die for

Lifting weights and eating lots of protein is one way to build muscle, but it takes time and effort. Some people take shortcuts to maximize the muscle they build by taking **steroids**. Steroids contain testosterone, which in large amounts has many dangerous side effects. The International Olympic Committee (IOC) bans steroids and regularly tests bodybuilders for such substances.

Using steroids is harmful and banned in all major competitive sports.

UNDER THE
-KNIFE -

Some people don't like the way their nose looks. Others think their ears are too big. To solve this, some people use cosmetic surgery to get the face they want.

Plastic surgery is almost as old as humans. Ancient Egyptian cosmetic surgeons were treating broken noses 5,000 years ago.

MAKE IT BETTER

In the past, plastic surgery was mainly used to correct facial and body defects that people were born with or that were caused by accidents. Plastic surgery advanced rapidly during World War I (1914–1918). The British surgeon Sir Harold Gillies carried out the first successful reconstruction of the face of a badly wounded soldier. He took skin from the soldier's body and used it to repair the soldier's damaged eyelids. Since then, huge advances in techniques have made plastic surgery far more successful for patients. This has created a valuable business, known as cosmetic surgery.

People undergo rhinoplasty, also known as a nose job, to change the size or shape of the nose.

I WANT TO LOOK BETTER!

Cosmetic surgery is surgery people choose to have to permanently change their appearance. Almost any part of the body can be changed with this kind of surgery, from faces to legs. Originally the United States led the emergence of cosmetic surgery, but it has been overtaken by Brazil. Brazil is the world center for cosmetic surgery, with around 5,500 certified surgeons. Face lifts continue to be popular in the United States.

For those who fear the surgeon's knife, there are temporary modern solutions to alter your appearance. Want to reduce the lines on your face without surgery? Try an injection of poison—better known as **Botox**. It does the trick!

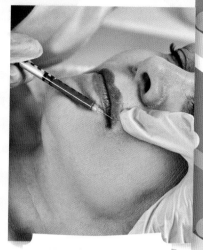

A physician injects a filler to keep a woman's lips plump.

to die for

As we age, our faces change. Wrinkles appear and the skin grows slack. Some people refuse to accept these changes. They have face lifts to try to keep them looking young. The surgeon lifts the skin and pulls it back to make it appear tauter. The procedure changes the way a person looks. The first time they look in the mirror might be a shock. Who's that person looking back at them?

A woman is prepared for Botox injections to reduce the appearance of wrinkles.

Chapter 6
THE TWENTY-FIRST
- CENTURY -

From applying makeup to permanent body changes such as tattoos and piercings, it is clear that many of us are not happy with the way we are!

Today millions of people modify their bodies by putting in earrings, having cosmetic surgery, or inking their skin. They may do so for cultural or religious reasons—as people have done throughout history.

ALL CHANGE!

In the Western world, however, there has been a huge rise in body modification for its own sake. Perhaps people are searching for a way to show they are unique among a global population of seven billion people. For some of them, the answer is to alter their appearance.

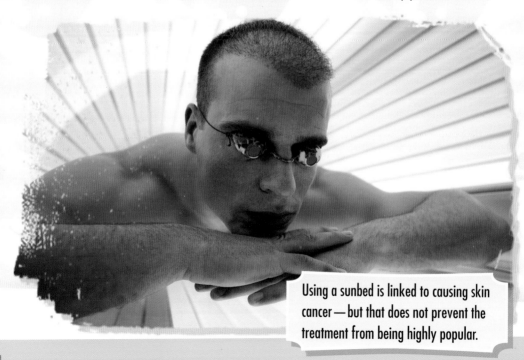

Using a sunbed is linked to causing skin cancer—but that does not prevent the treatment from being highly popular.

Around 4 million Americans wear braces at any time in an attempt to make their teeth straighter and more even.

One temporary way some people achieve this is to get a suntan in winter, when most people have pale skin. A more permanent way one might make their looks more distinctive is to have a face lift.

IS THERE A PROBLEM?

Body modification is now so widespread that many practices have become socially acceptable. In fact, a practice such as having your teeth straightened or whitened is not only socially acceptable, but having bad teeth is now considered socially unacceptable to many people. Losing weight in order to change body shape is approved of, but gaining large amounts of weight is not. Foot binding is now illegal in China, but across the globe people squeeze their feet into ill-fitting shoes that leave the feet deformed. Having fillers injected into lips to make them fuller is a popular practice among lots of women in the West, but lip enlargement as practiced in Africa is not so popular in the West. Confusing, isn't it?

INK
- FEST -

Only a few decades ago, tattoos were seen as an extreme form of body decoration. Now they are mainstream. Every major city has a tattoo parlor.

Tattoos have come a long way (literally) since Polynesians and the Maori of New Zealand perfected the art of inking their bodies and faces. Tattoos have long been a way of expressing both individuality and membership in different groups.

PAINTED PEOPLE

Tattooing is the most popular way for many people to decorate their bodies. In the past, tattoos were hidden away under clothing. Today tattoos are on full display. Some people even have them on their necks and faces. Tattoos have become so mainstream that many employers no longer ban them.

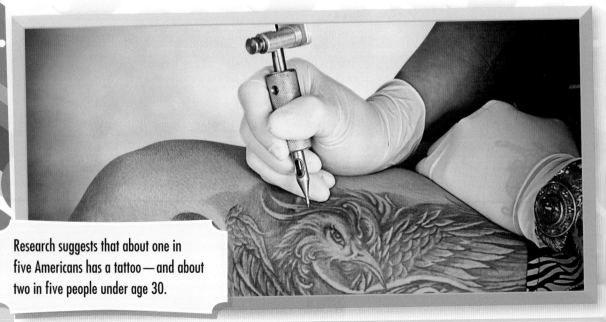

Research suggests that about one in five Americans has a tattoo — and about two in five people under age 30.

to die for

Once people have a tattoo, how about a few body piercings? Piercing ears and noses has become so commonplace that people now often pierce their tongues, nipples, eyebrows, noses, and belly buttons to be that bit different. The most pierced woman in the world, the Brazilian-born Elaine Davidson, is said to have almost 10,000 piercings all over her body. That must have hurt!

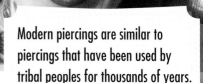

Modern piercings are similar to piercings that have been used by tribal peoples for thousands of years.

WHAT'S THE RISK?

Tattoos might be everywhere—but so are permanent mistakes. Bad artists might not be able to draw, and there are many examples where they make spelling mistakes in tattoos. Worse still, they might use industrial-grade printer ink or automobile paint, which are cheaper than tattoo ink but can cause infection. Hygiene is crucial in a tattoo parlor. A failure to **sterilize** needles correctly can spread infectious diseases such as Hepatitis B and C or HIV. It's for that reason that blood donation centers often ask people who have a tattoo to wait a year before donating blood.

Despite the risks, it seems that tattooing will remain popular. People remain happy to be permanently drawn on, to go under the surgeon's knife, or to pierce their skin. Just as they have for centuries, people are willing to modify their bodies in return for feeling that bit more special.

-TIMELINE-

c. 3300 BC	Ötzi the Iceman dies in central Europe. His skin is tattooed over the joints.
c. 2000 BC	Egyptian mummies are buried with tattoos.
c. 2000 BC	The Chinchorro of Chile practice head elongation.
AD 300s	The Emperor Constantine forbids tattoos in the Roman Empire.
900s	A courtier named Yao Niang is said to have introduced foot binding at the emperor's court in China.
c. 1000	The Anasazi of what is now the southwestern United States practice head flattening.
1470	Queen Juana of Portugal wears a stomacher with a farthingale to disguise the fact that she is pregnant.
1500s	European men start stuffing their doublets with bombast.
1537	King Henry VIII of England is painted wearing a doublet stuffed with bombast.
1610	English playwright William Shakespeare is painted wearing an earring.
1769	British sailor Captain James Cook sees tattoos when he visits Tahiti in the Pacific Ocean.
1811	Friedrich Ludwig Jahn introduces the first modern gymnasium in Europe.
1829	European women wear crinolines made of horsehair beneath their skirts.
1840s	Victorian women start wearing devices called corsets to compress their waists.

1840s	Drugstores in the United States increasingly hire cosmeticians.
1850s	Crinolines evolve into cages of steel hoops.
1870	Europe's first tattoo parlor opens in London.
1881	A fashion emerges for wearing bustles, which push the skirts back behind the wearer.
1881	The Duke of York, later King George VI, becomes the first member of the British royal family to have a tattoo.
1888	An American man is strangled to death by his shirt collar.
1893	Bodybuilder Eugene Sandow appears at the world exposition in Chicago.
1908	French fashion designer Paul Poiret introduces the hobble skirt, which prevents women from walking naturally.
1914–1918	During World War I, great advances are made in plastic surgery.
1920s	Charles Atlas successfully markets his bodybuilding business in the United States.
1950s	Tight jeans worn with high-heeled shoes or winklepickers become fashionable for young women and men, respectively.
2012	One in five of all Americans has a tattoo. Among those under age 30, the figure is two in five.

-GLOSSARY-

arthritis a medical condition that causes pain in body joints

Ayurvedic related to the traditional Hindu system of medicine

bodice the part of a woman's dress above the waist (not including the sleeves)

body modification the deliberate alteration of one's appearance, particularly with permanent changes

bombast a mixture of light fibers and other materials used to stuff clothes

Botox a drug used to remove the look of facial wrinkles

bunions painful swellings on the big toe

corset a tight-fitting undergarment worn between the chest and the hips to compress the body

courtier a companion to a king or queen in a royal court

crinoline a stiffened underskirt or frame worn to make a skirt stand out from the legs

doublets short, close-fitting men's jackets

fertility the ability to have children

glacier a slowly moving mass of ice

harem pants soft, loose-fitting pants that are gathered at the waist and ankles

incisions decorative cuts made into a surface

lice tiny bloodsucking insects

lotus a water lily with a large flower

mehndi temporary tattoos applied in India

milestones significant stages or events in life

misaligned in an incorrect position

missionaries people sent to other countries to do religious work

mohair yarn made from the wool of angora goats

mummies dried and preserved bodies of the dead

nobles people belonging to the elite class of society

petticoats lightweight undergarments worn beneath a skirt or dress

pleats folds of fabric stitched into a garment

Romanticism an artistic movement that celebrated intense feelings and beauty in nature

sterilize to make something free from bacteria

steroids artificial compounds that are used to build muscles

stiletto a very thin, tall heel on a woman's shoe

tattoos designs drawn onto the skin and made permanent by pushing ink into the skin

trance a semiconscious, dreamlike mental state

vanity the quality of having too much pride in one's own appearance

voluminous very loose and full

-FOR MORE INFORMATION-

BOOKS

Bailey, Diane. *Tattoo Art Around the World*. New York, NY: Rosen Publishing Group, 2012.

Baum, Margaux, and Margaret Scott. *Fashion and Clothing*. New York, NY: Rosen Central, 2017.

Gordon, Stephen G. *Expressing the Inner Wild: Tattoos, Piercing, Jewelry, and Other Body Art*. Minneapolis, MN: Twenty-First Century Books, 2014.

Keyser, Amber J. *Underneath It All: A History of Women's Underwear*. Minneapolis, MN: Twenty-First Century Books, 2018.

Park, Louise. *Extreme Fashions*. New York, NY: Rosen Publishing Group, 2013.

WEBSITES

History of Women's Corsets
www.fashionintime.org/history-of-womens-corsets-part-1
This site includes a comprehensive history of the use of corsets.

How Tattoos Work
health.howstuffworks.com/skin-care/beauty/skin-and-lifestyle/tattoo.htm
Read an explanation of tattooing and related health and legal issues here.

Scarification
kids.kiddle.co/Scarification
This page features an introduction to the practice of scarification.

Publisher's note to educators and parents: Our editors have carefully reviewed these websites to ensure that they are suitable for students. Many websites change frequently, however, and we cannot guarantee that a site's future contents will continue to meet our high standards of quality and educational value. Be advised that students should be closely supervised whenever they access the Internet.

-INDEX-